UNICORN ACADEMY

Matilda followed Pearl's gaze and she gasped. A figure cloaked in black was cantering toward the clearing on a golden-maned unicorn. Matilda climbed onto Pearl's back, but it was too late for them to escape. She gripped Pearl's mane. "What are we going to do now?" she whispered.

★ ★ ★

LOOK OUT FOR MORE ADVENTURES AT

UNICORN ACADEMY

Sophia and Rainbow

Scarlett and Blaze

Ava and Star

Isabel and Cloud

Layla and Dancer

Olivia and Snowflake

Rosa and Crystal

Ariana and Whisper

Matilda and Pearl

Freya and Honey

Violet and Twinkle

★ ★ ★

UNICORN ACADEMY
Matilda and Pearl

JULIE SYKES
illustrated by LUCY TRUMAN

A STEPPING STONE BOOK™
Random House 🏠 New York

Text copyright © 2019 by Julie Sykes and Linda Chapman
Cover art and interior illustrations copyright © 2019 by Lucy Truman

Visit us on the Web! rhcbooks.com

Educators and librarians, for a variety of teaching tools, visit us at
RHTeachersLibrarians.com

Library of Congress Cataloging-in-Publication Data
Names: Sykes, Julie, author. | Truman, Lucy, illustrator.
Title: Matilda and Pearl / Julie Sykes ; illustrated by Lucy Truman.
Description: First American edition. |
New York : Random House Children's Books, [2020] |
Series: Unicorn Academy ; 9 | "A Stepping Stone Book." |
Audience: Ages 6-9. | Summary: During a camping trip, fun-loving but
disorganized Matilda fears letting down her friends, but her unicorn, Pearl, finds
her magic in time to protect them all from a malicious, cloaked figure.
Identifiers: LCCN 2020013026 (print) | LCCN 2020013027 (ebook) |
ISBN 978-0-593-30623-9 (trade paperback) |
ISBN 978-0-593-30624-6 (lib. bdg.) | ISBN 978-0-593-30625-3 (ebook)
Subjects: CYAC: Unicorns—Fiction. | Magic—Fiction. | Friendship—
Fiction. | Boarding schools—Fiction. | Schools—Fiction.
Classification: LCC PZ7.S98325 Mat 2020 (print) | LCC PZ7.S98325 (ebook)
DDC [Fic]—dc23

Printed in the United States of America
10 9 8 7 6 5 4 3 2 1
First American Edition

For the very magical
Philippa and Polly

CHAPTER 1

"Pearl, you moved!" Matilda was trying to draw Pearl, her unicorn, but it wasn't going too well. "Your leg is all wrong in my picture now. Pleeeease stand still."

"Sorry, Matilda. I just can't stop thinking about magic. When do you think I'll get mine, and what do you think it will be?" Pearl tossed her pink, yellow, and purple mane.

"I don't know," said Matilda, re-sketching Pearl's leg.

Pearl began to spin in circles. "Maybe I'll be able to make a snow twister like Crystal!" She spun faster until she almost tripped over her hooves. Slowing down, she tilted her head and got a dreamy look on her face. "Or I might get soothing magic like Whisper. Or what about freezing magic?" Pearl held the pose like a statue. "Nah. Freezing magic is boring! I wouldn't mind getting wind magic, though, like Golden Briar. Wouldn't it be fun to have wind magic, Matilda?" Pearl blew out through her nostrils, making a loud trumpeting sound. She crossed her eyes and blew so hard it made her cheeks wobble. "Or flying magic! Imagine if I had wings!" She leaped into the air with her hooves pointed.

"Pearl! Stop goofing around so I can finish this picture!" Matilda tried to look angry, but Pearl looked so funny that she started to giggle. Her pencil scratched across her sketch pad as she tried to capture the dancing unicorn.

Pearl began prancing around the field, tapping

flowers with a hoof and making a popping, crackling noise. "Guess what magic now, Matilda?"

"Fire magic," said Matilda.

"And now?" Pearl walked very slowly, lifting each hoof in a tiptoe.

"Stop!" Matilda chuckled and dropped her pencil. "How can I draw anything when you keep making me laugh? What sort of magic is that supposed to be? Whatever it is, I hope you don't get it. You look like a circus pony!"

Pearl trotted over and rested her head on Matilda's shoulder, nuzzling her dark red hair. "I don't mind what magic I have. I just wish I could find it," she said, blinking her long eyelashes. "It's summer already. We're halfway through our time at Unicorn Academy. What if I don't find out before the graduation ball in December? And we haven't bonded, either."

All the unicorns at Unicorn Academy were trying to discover their magic power and bond with their rider. When a rider and unicorn bonded, a strand of the rider's hair turned the same color as their unicorn's mane. Matilda couldn't wait for a pink-and-yellow streak to appear in her long red hair. She was sure it would soon. She and Pearl had been best friends ever since their first day at the academy when Ms. Nettles, the head teacher, had paired them up. At first, Ms. Nettles hadn't seemed sure about it.

"I hope you're not going to be a bad influence on each other," she'd said, frowning behind her glasses. "Since you're both quite disorganized, maybe I should put you with someone else?"

Matilda remembered how she'd crossed her fingers tightly behind her back, hoping that Ms. Nettles would keep her and Pearl together. She'd loved Pearl from first sight. Pearl's dark eyes seemed to twinkle playfully, and she was perfect for drawing too. Her beautiful white coat was patterned with colorful and interesting shapes.

"Do you think Ms. Nettles was right? Are we a bad influence on each other?" asked Matilda, straightening her glasses on her nose and remembering the head teacher's words. Maybe that was why they hadn't found Pearl's magic and bonded yet.

"Definitely not!" Pearl declared. "We're perfect for each other!" She shook her head. "Just imagine if I'd been paired with Ariana. Nightmare!"

Matilda giggled. "Ariana's not that bad. She's just a lot more organized than us. I've been getting along much better with her since our adventure in the woods."

"That was fun, wasn't it? I loved playing in the river and solving the mystery." Pearl bucked across the meadow as she remembered.

"Whoa! Pearl, steady," Ariana called out as she came running across the grass toward them. "You're going to kick someone if you do that. Matilda! Did you forget that Ms. Nettles wants to talk to us about the camping trip and scavenger hunt?"

Matilda caught her breath. "I thought the meeting was tomorrow."

"No, we leave for the trip tomorrow," said

Ariana. "You never listen. The meeting's starting soon. I've been trying to find you."

"Wait!" Matilda looked at the picture she had been drawing and snorted with laughter. "Look at my picture, Pearl!"

Pearl trotted over. "You've given me wings!" She giggled. "I look very strange. Why did you do that?"

Matilda frowned. "I have no idea. I thought I was just drawing what I was seeing."

"I didn't have wings last time I looked," said Pearl, glancing over her shoulder. "Nope, no wings."

"Come on, Matilda," said Ariana impatiently. "Diamond dorm will all be in trouble if we arrive late."

"I'll see you after your meeting, Matilda," said Pearl. She trotted off toward the stables.

Matilda set off with Ariana, but halfway across the field, she stopped. "My pencils and water bottle! Where are they? Did you pick them up for me, Ariana?"

"No, why would I?" asked Ariana.

"I'll have to go back for them," Matilda said, turning around.

Ariana groaned. "Why are you so forgetful?"

Matilda swept her long red hair over her shoulders and hurried back to get her stuff. But after running a few steps, she spotted a bright yellow butterfly flitting from flower to flower. She stopped to examine it.

"Matilda!" exclaimed Ariana. "Come on!"

Matilda sighed and left the butterfly. Ariana needed to chill. So what if they were a bit late? They wouldn't get into that much trouble. She gathered her things into her arms and headed back toward Ariana, the pile wobbling unsteadily. "Here, hold this for me." Matilda handed Ariana a water bottle.

Ariana pursed her lips, but she took the water bottle and a packet of pencils as it started to slide from on top of Matilda's sketch pad. "You're so disorganized."

Matilda shrugged. Being organized was hard work, and she only liked to work hard at things she enjoyed—like drawing. "So?" she said. "It doesn't matter."

Ariana gave her an annoyed look. "It does! It's good to be organized. Remember our adventure in the woods when the animals turned bad because the waterfall was blocked? We might not have been able to start the waterfall flowing again if I hadn't been prepared and brought a load of stuff with me."

"I suppose," Matilda said.

"Now, we need to get to the meeting and find out how we can prepare for this scavenger hunt and camping trip," said Ariana. She shook her head. "I know it's supposed to be a treat, but I'm very surprised the teachers are allowing it. They still don't know who was responsible for the waterfall drying up. You'd think they'd be doing more to try to find out who it was. What if that person strikes again?"

Matilda stared at her. Ariana really did worry about silly things. The teachers always had everything under control. Matilda felt sorry for her anxious friend. She really needed to laugh more. Seeing a beetle on the path ahead of them, she suddenly had an idea. She knew exactly how to get Ariana giggling. She stopped and pointed at the beetle.

"Eeek! Watch out!" she squealed. "It's a

three-headed snotty-nose flapdoodle!" She jumped sideways into a bed of sparkle lilies, dragging Ariana with her.

"What? That thing there?" Ariana gasped, clinging to Matilda's arm. "Is it dangerous?"

Matilda burst out laughing. "Joke!" she exclaimed. "There's no such thing as a three-headed snotty-nose flapdoodle. I just made it up! Your face was so funny, Ariana!"

Ariana glared at her. "Matilda!"

"Girls! Get off those flowers immediately," a voice shouted. "What do you think you are doing?"

Ariana jumped off the flowerbed as Ms.

Bramble, the grumpy head gardener, came stomping up with Ms. Willow, the school nurse. "Sorry!" she gasped as the gardener looked at them angrily.

"It was my fault," said Matilda, not wanting to get Ariana in trouble.

"I don't care whose fault it is!" snapped Ms. Bramble. "Guardians of the island are supposed to look after all of nature—animals and plants— and you have both just squashed four lilies! Honestly! I've got my hands full with a quiverleaf tree dying without you squashing lilies too!"

"I'm so, so sorry," said Ariana.

Matilda felt bad as she looked at the broken lilies. "Yes, me too." She hadn't meant to ruin the flowerbed.

"I'm sure it was just an accident," Ms. Willow said, tucking a loose strand of hair back into her neat bun. She was younger than Ms. Bramble, and her eyes were kind. "You'll be more careful in the future, won't you, girls?"

Matilda and Ariana nodded.

Ms. Willow smiled at them. "Then we'll say no more about it. Off you run."

Ms. Bramble harrumphed and went over to the quiverleaf tree that stood behind the lilies. Matilda noticed that its branches were drooping and its leaves were turning brown. Ms. Bramble was carrying a large bucket and a length of green bandage, and Ms. Willow held a small silver knife. Matilda watched them curiously. What were they doing?

Ariana tugged Matilda by the sleeve. "Come on."

"Coming," said Matilda, her eyes still on the gardener and the school nurse. It was an odd combination of people. What exactly were they going to do with a bucket and a knife?

CHAPTER 2

Ariana hurried on, but Matilda stood, staring, as Ms. Bramble pressed the point of the knife to the tree and made a small, deep cut in its trunk. Pale liquid oozed out. Ms. Willow stepped forward, soaking it up with some cotton. She asked Ms. Bramble to hold the cotton against the tree. From her small black medicine bag, she brought out a syringe and a bottle filled with a green liquid. Shaking the bottle, she unscrewed the top and drew the liquid up into the syringe. The liquid was greener than fresh peas and very sparkly. Matilda caught the scent of something sweet and minty.

Ms. Willow asked Ms. Bramble to remove the wad of cotton from the tree trunk and then she stuck the syringe into the cut. Slowly and carefully, Ms. Willow began to inject the sparkly green liquid into the tree.

Matilda couldn't contain her curiosity for a second longer. "What are you doing?"

Ms. Bramble swung around. Matilda braced herself, expecting to get in trouble. But Ms. Willow broke in before Ms. Bramble could speak.

"It's good to see a future guardian of Unicorn Island taking an interest in its wildlife," Ms. Willow said with a warm smile. "This quiverleaf tree is dying. I'm hoping that my special remedy will heal it. The medicine has to be injected into the tree. It's tricky to do. I'm showing Ms. Bramble how to do it so that if there's a next time, she can do it herself."

"Is that what's in the syringe? The medicine?" asked Matilda.

"Yes, it is. Once I've finished injecting it, I'll bandage the tree trunk to stop the medicine from leaking back out with the tree's sap. The bandage also protects the tree by preventing germs from entering the cut."

"That's very interesting," said Ariana, who'd

come back for Matilda. She gave Matilda's arm a tug. "But we really have to go."

"Of course! Off you run!" Ms. Willow smiled as she flapped her hands, cheerfully shooing them away.

Matilda and Ariana ran all the way to the hall, arriving just as Ms. Nettles walked onto the stage. The rest of the school were already in their seats, whispering together. The hall was one of Matilda's favorite places in the school. It had a domed glass roof that was filled with colorful swirls. In the center of the room was a magical map—a three-dimensional model of the island that could transport people anywhere they wanted to go. It was protected by a glimmering force field. At the far end, the huge stage overlooked the room.

"There you are! We thought you were going to miss it," said Rosa, squeezing up next to Violet to make space for them. Freya was at the far end of the group, her blond head bent over as she scribbled in her notebook. She loved to invent things and was working on a new idea. She hadn't told the rest of Diamond dorm what it was going to be yet, but she seemed to be spending more and more time lost in her own thoughts.

"Listen carefully, everyone," said Ms. Nettles.

"This is your first camping trip, and there are a lot of things that you need to know. You'll be going to Dingleberry Dell—a wooded area at the base of the mountains. It's a short ride from the school grounds."

Matilda concentrated for a whole minute before her mind started to wander. It was very hard to pay attention when there were so many things she wanted to draw. Almost without realizing it, Matilda's fingers reached for her favorite pencil, which she had poked in her thick red hair. While Ms. Nettles talked about tents and sleeping bags, Matilda began to draw the hall in her sketch pad. Her pencil flew across the paper, sketching the grandness of the room and how the domed glass roof filled the space with a soft rainbow light. By her side, Ariana was making notes, nodding to herself and underlining the important points. Finally, Ms. Nettles finished.

"I wish we could go camping right now. I don't think I can wait until tomorrow," said Rosa as they all left the hall.

"Me neither," Violet agreed. "I hope we're allowed to toast food over the campfire. My uncle sent me a bag of chocolate bread. It's even more delicious when it's toasted."

"Yummy," Matilda said, looking up. "I love camping. Food tastes so much better when you cook it outdoors."

Ariana frowned. "We'll have to be careful to cook everything well or we might get sick. And what about cleaning up? I think I'll add an extra bucket to my packing list."

"I wish we didn't have to go camping," sighed Freya. "What?" she added, seeing Matilda's confused stare. "Imagine this: you're drawing something special and you really want to finish it. Would you want to go camping then? This thing I'm working on—my invention—I've just reached the exciting bit where I'm ready to start building it. If the camping trip was next week, then I wouldn't mind. But this week, I just want to stay behind and build."

"We're only away for one night," said Violet. "You'll be back before you know it. And no one will get sick, Ariana."

"Bring your invention with you. I'm going to take my sketch pad," said Matilda.

Freya shook her head. "Can't," she said. "It's too big."

"So if Matilda is busy drawing and Freya is making notes on her invention, does that mean the rest of us get stuck with putting up all the tents?" asked Rosa. "If it does, then watch out, you two. We might just put some bugs in your bed."

"And spiders in your slippers," Violet added.

Ariana shuddered. She hated spiders.

"Worms in your wash bag," Rosa giggled. "Beetles in your boots."

"Oooh, yes please. I want bugs, spiders, and worms. Don't put beetles in my boots, though, in case I squish one by accident." Matilda laughed. She loved a good adventure, and nothing was going to put her off the camping trip. Not even the thought of bugs in her bed. It sounded way too exciting! She skipped ahead and ducked behind a statue of a unicorn when no one was looking. Hidden behind the statue, she wrapped her arms around her chest, hugging herself tightly to stop the laughter spilling out as her friends' voices drew closer.

"BOO!" Matilda jumped out, flapping her arms and leaping around. "I'm a vampire bat.

I only come out at night.
Run before I
bite you with
my fangs!"

"Aaarrgh!"
shrieked Ariana.

"Matilda!" Violet put
a hand over her heart.
"You scared me!"

"What if there are
vampire bats in the dell?"
asked Ariana. "Or other dangerous creatures."

"Then we'll chase them away, of course," said
Matilda with a shrug.

"Yeah!" said Rosa, high-fiving her. "We're not
scared! Diamond dorm are strong and tough.
Diamond dorm forever!"

CHAPTER 3

Matilda was so sleepy she could hardly keep her eyes open. She'd had a busy day and was looking forward to getting into bed, but first she had to find her pajamas. They weren't under her pillow or blanket, but there was a pile of clothes on the floor. Matilda prodded it with her toe. Perhaps the pajamas were in there somewhere? Ariana came over, and Matilda got ready for a lecture. Ariana had every reason to be annoyed about the mess as it had spilled onto her side of the room, but Ariana was focused on something else. She handed a piece of paper to Matilda.

"Okay, I've made a list of the things we all need to take on the camping trip. There's one here for each of you," she added, handing them around.

"Thanks, Ariana," the other girls said.

"Yeah, thanks," said Matilda, looking at the paper. Where did Ariana get it from? It was perfect for drawing on—just the right thickness and with a lovely smooth surface. Matilda's fingers twitched as she looked for a pencil. She found one tucked behind her ear. Flipping the list over, Matilda began to sketch. First she drew Pearl mid-leap, then she gave the unicorn large, graceful wings. She added a sky filled with fluffy clouds for Pearl to fly through. *It would be amazing if Pearl had flying magic,* she thought, smiling to herself.

"Matilda!" Ariana said.

Matilda's pencil skidded across the page. She

looked up. "What?" Why was Ariana looking so upset?

"You've drawn on the list, and I bet you haven't even read it!"

"So?" Matilda said, shrugging. "If I forget something, it's no big deal. You all will help me out."

"What if we can't help you? Say you forget something important and nobody has an extra one?" The words poured from Ariana. "Why is everything just a huge joke to you? Don't you remember our last trip? What if the person who blocked the waterfall turns up and does more dark magic?"

Violet put a hand on Ariana's arm. "There hasn't been any trouble since then. You shouldn't worry about it."

Matilda nodded. She didn't like seeing Ariana so unhappy. "Violet's right. The teachers wouldn't let us go if there was any danger. You worry too much, Ariana."

Ariana bit her lip and sat down on her bed.

Rosa started to brush her long, dark hair. "Wouldn't it be great if we could figure out who it was? Ms. Nettles and the other teachers would be so happy!"

"But how can we possibly figure it out when the teachers haven't?" said Freya, glancing up from her notebook. "It's not going to happen, Rosa."

"Who knows? Maybe we will find something to help us solve the mystery while we're out camping," said Rosa.

"Oh yes," said Matilda, her eyes gleaming at the idea.

"No," said Violet firmly, glancing at Ariana's alarmed face. "This is just going to be a fun little camping trip. There'll be no mysteries, no adventures, and absolutely no danger."

Matilda caught Rosa's eye and knew what she was thinking right away—mysteries, adventures, and danger sounded like fun!

★

The following morning, Matilda was the last to leave the dorm room. She hurried after her friends, who had gone to prepare their unicorns long before her. She'd packed her backpack in a hurry, shoving everything in, and now something hard was sticking into her back. *I should probably repack it when I get to the stables,* thought Matilda, but when she got there, she had so much fun brushing and talking to Pearl that she forgot.

"So, tell me about this camping trip." Pearl nudged Matilda, then blew in her hair to make her giggle.

"Well," said Matilda, trying to remember what Ms. Nettles had said. "Once we get to the dell, we're supposed to find somewhere good to make a camp. There's also a scavenger hunt with a prize for the winning team."

"I hope Diamond dorm win the scavenger hunt!" said Pearl eagerly.

"Me too," said Matilda, going to the stable door to fetch Pearl's breakfast. "I bet we have a good chance of winning."

"Huh! In your dreams!" said snooty Valentina,

who was coming out of her unicorn's stable. "Ruby dorm have already found half the things on the list. You'll never beat us!"

"But that's cheating!" protested Matilda. "We're supposed to find the things in the dell. You're not allowed to start the scavenger hunt until we get there."

Valentina smiled smugly. "Whatever."

Matilda glared at her. Horrid Valentina. She looked like a frog with her big bulgy eyes and wide smile. Matilda could feel a picture coming on. She whipped out a pencil and her mini sketch pad from her pants pocket. She drew Valentina standing with her arms crossed and a very stuck-up expression on her face, unaware that a frog was sitting on her head.

Valentina walked up and looked over Matilda's shoulder.

"Really, Matilda," she said, looking at the drawing down her long nose. "Is that your best work? Who's it supposed to be, then? You can't draw, and you're going to lose the scavenger hunt for Diamond dorm. Look at you. You've lost half your camping stuff already!" Valentina pointed at Matilda's backpack. She had put it on the floor by the stable door and it had fallen over, spilling the things inside. "I feel sorry for the rest of Diamond dorm. I'm very glad you're not on my team!"

Her words stung, and Matilda flushed. "I wouldn't want to be on your team anyway," she said.

Valentina smiled meanly. "You know, I really

don't know how your dorm put up with you. I bet they wish they had someone else instead." She saw Matilda's red face. "Aw, have I upset the little baby?"

"No. I was just thinking how lucky your dorm are," said Matilda. Valentina blinked in surprise. Matilda's hand flew across the page, changing her drawing, giving Valentina the head of a big frog. "Because if we have to collect a tree frog in the scavenger hunt, your team will have one already!" she said, holding the picture up.

Rosa emerged from Crystal's stable. She laughed out loud when she saw the drawing.

Valentina scowled. "You're a loser, Matilda! And we'll see who's laughing at the end of the day!" She stormed away.

Rosa giggled. "Oh dear, I think you upset her. What a pity!" Her eyes sparkled.

Matilda went to Pearl's stable and shoved

everything back into her backpack.

"Are you okay?" Pearl asked. Matilda turned
and hugged her. Pearl nuzzled Matilda's hair.
"Your eyes are all glittery."

Matilda bit her lip. She was more upset by
Valentina's words than she wanted to say, but she

knew she could tell Pearl anything. "You don't think she's right, do you, Pearl?" she whispered. "That the others are wishing I wasn't on their team?"

"Absolutely not!" Pearl blew on her cheek. "Don't listen to Valentina. She's just being mean."

"I try not to listen when Valentina's not nice." Matilda managed a small smile as she stroked Pearl's soft face. But once mean words were out, it was hard to ignore them.

There was the sound of a whistle blowing outside. Rosa popped her head around the stable door. "Come on, Matilda!" she cried excitedly. "Ms. Nettles wants to talk to us!"

CHAPTER 4

Everyone gathered together in the yard for last-minute instructions. Ms. Nettles stood on a mounting block with Ms. Rivers, the strict Geography and Culture teacher who was going with the students. Ms. Nettles clapped her hands to get everyone's attention. When the yard was totally silent, she began.

"There are a few important things you must pay attention to before you leave. Firstly, the scavenger hunt competition: the winner is the first team back with everything on the list. That's the whole team. Ms. Rivers will be camping at the entrance to Dingleberry Dell and her tent is your finishing point.

"Secondly, and more importantly," she continued, "though I know you all want to win the competition, do not put the scavenger hunt ahead of pitching your tent. You must make sure that you are all able to sleep safely tonight! And pick your campsite carefully. Last year, some students pitched their tent on an anthill." Her lips twitched as she waited for the laughter to fade. "They did not have a comfortable night's sleep! And don't leave putting up your tent until dark. Pitching a tent at night is almost impossible. Finally, no magic can be used in the scavenger hunt." Ms. Nettles silenced the groans by waving her hand. "Many unicorns have still not found their magic. The scavenger hunt should be fair, especially since the prize for winning is something very special."

"What is it?" asked Miki from Topaz dorm.

"You'll have to wait and see, Miki," Ms. Nettles said mysteriously. "Better still, you'll have to win and see! Now, Ms. Rivers will lead the way to the dell. Go and get your unicorns! There's a scavenger hunt to win!"

A loud cheer rang out, sending the bluebirds perched on the fence fluttering up with alarmed squawks.

★

The sun was shining, and it was a lovely ride to the dell. The mountains rose up behind the cluster of trees, tall and craggy, their peaks standing against the sapphire-blue sky. At the entrance to the dell stood a tree that had turned completely white. The other trees were in a thick group behind it, with birds singing and squirrels hopping from branch to branch.

"That white tree was once struck by lightning,

children. It's easy to spot, and I shall camp here,"
Ms. Rivers told the students. "When you have
completed the scavenger hunt, come and find me.
Now, off you all go!"

Everyone whooped and ran into the trees. At

first there were students and unicorns everywhere,
but slowly they all separated, following different
paths. Rosa led the way for Diamond dorm.
"Let's get far away from everyone else!" she said,
heading for the center of the dell.

They cantered through the trees, their unicorns leaping over roots and stones on the track. At last, when the noise from the other students had faded and they were completely alone, Rosa and Crystal stopped in a grassy clearing. "Okay, let's look at the list," Rosa said. Each team had been given a list of things they had to find in the dell. Everyone crowded around as Rosa read the piece of paper.

"It says we need a green feather, a six-petal daisy, an orange leaf, something pink, a sparkly hag stone—that's a stone with a hole in the middle—and a sprig of red heather," she said. "Should we get started?"

"I think we should set up our camp first," said Ariana. "Let's put the tents up before it gets dark, like Ms. Nettles told us to."

"But it won't be dark for ages," argued Rosa.

"I know. Why don't we find some of the things

on the list and then find somewhere to camp?" suggested Violet.

"But if we want to win the scavenger hunt, we should find all the things first," Rosa disagreed.

As they continued to argue about what to do, Matilda pulled out her sketch pad and started to draw the trees around her. It was a very pretty clearing, with a sparkling stream running through it and pink and purple flowers growing around the base of the trees. She was drawing a squirrel when she realized that Rosa was talking to her.

"Matilda! Did you hear what I just asked? We're taking a vote. Are you in or out?"

"In or out of what?" said Matilda in confusion.

Rosa frowned. "Honestly, Matilda. You never listen, do you? We're voting on whether we should find somewhere to camp or look for the things on the list first."

"Oh." Matilda frowned. "Well, why don't we just camp here and then start looking for the scavenger hunt stuff?"

The others looked around. "I suppose this would be a good place to camp," said Ariana thoughtfully. "It's got a stream for water, and it's flat and sheltered."

"And look!" Violet jumped off Twinkle and ran to a clump of round, red-tipped bushes. "Red heather!" she said, pulling a sprig off. "It's one of the things we need. We might find some of the other things right here too! Good idea, Matilda."

"I suppose we could camp here, but we can't spend too long putting up our tents," said Rosa. "I want to win this contest!" She got off Crystal. "Come on, everyone. Be as quick as you can!"

Matilda dismounted and caught sight of

a large black-and-white bird perched on a rock by the stream, watching for fish. Her fingers itched to draw it, but she stopped herself. She still remembered Valentina's words and she didn't want to be the reason why Diamond dorm lost the scavenger hunt.

Everyone had a hard time pitching the tents.

"Now to make it look homey," said Ariana, when the brightly colored tents were finally up. "Let's unpack our backpacks and get our sleeping bags out." Her sleeping bag was tied to her backpack in a neat roll.

Matilda looked at it and then looked at her own backpack. Her heart sank into her boots.

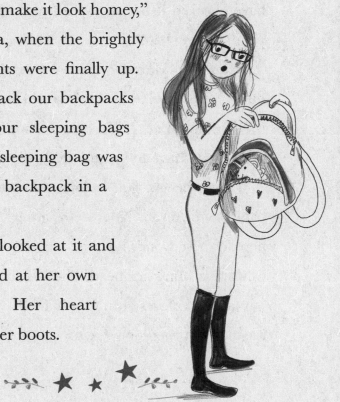

"Oh no!" she groaned. "I haven't got my sleeping bag. It came untied when I dropped my backpack in Pearl's stable. I meant to tie it back on, but I forgot."

Ariana put her hands on her hips. "Matilda, this is just not funny. This is why I gave you a list. If you hadn't scribbled all over it, maybe you'd have checked it before we left and remembered your sleeping bag!"

"Honestly, Matilda! We'll lose the scavenger hunt if we have to go back to the academy for it." Rosa scowled. "You heard what Ms. Nettles said; we all have to finish together."

"I can't believe you've forgotten your sleeping bag!" said Freya. "Now we're going to be stuck here in these woods for even longer."

Matilda hung her head. She hardly ever cried, but now her eyes stung with tears. She hadn't meant to let everyone down.

Violet hurried over to her. "Look, don't worry. We can go back and get it, and if we lose the competition, well, so what? We'll still have fun camping."

Rosa's annoyed face left Matilda knowing what she thought of that. She quickly rubbed her eyes. She didn't want the others to see she was crying.

"It's okay," she said, turning away quickly so they couldn't see. "I'll just sleep on that heather over there."

"But it's not very soft," said Violet in concern.

"I don't mind," said Matilda, carrying her backpack over to the heather. A sweet smell of burnt sugar wafted toward her. She sniffed in surprise.

"Matilda." Pearl urgently nudged her hand. "Your sleeping bag is over there— Look!"

Matilda followed her gaze and saw a dark

purple sleeping bag lying near the heather. Relief shot through her. She must have brought it with her after all and just dropped it as they entered the clearing!

Matilda jogged toward it, but as she drew closer, the bag seemed to vanish and change into a dark purple bush. She pulled up in surprise. What had just happened?

"It's gone!" Pearl was just as confused.

Matilda's brow furrowed. That was the second time she'd seen something that wasn't there. First there were the wings that she'd drawn on Pearl in her picture, and now the sleeping bag that was actually a plant. Maybe she needed her eyes checked? But Pearl had seen the sleeping bag too. What was going on?

"Hey, Matilda," called Violet. "I have a good idea. Remember that lesson we had with Ms. Rivers on the Heart Tree?"

Matilda screwed up her eyes as she did her best to remember. "The oldest tree on the island?" she ventured.

"That's the one. Well, it's right here, in the middle of the dell."

"Don't lots of pink chinchillas live in its branches?" Matilda remembered.

"Yes," said Rosa. "Over the Heart Tree's lifetime, it's absorbed lots of magic from the island. Pink chinchillas are drawn to magic and made their home there centuries ago."

"And . . . chinchillas molt this time of year!" Violet smiled. "Their fur is super soft, and we need something pink for the scavenger hunt. If we could find some pink chinchilla fur, we could take some for the scavenger hunt and some for you to put on the heather to make it softer." She looked at Rosa. "What do you think?"

47

"It's a great idea!" said Rosa, high-fiving her. "And on the way to the Heart Tree, we can look for more of the scavenger hunt things. Let's go!"

Matilda breathed a sigh of relief. Maybe she hadn't ruined the hunt for everyone after all!

CHAPTER 5

Matilda and Pearl rode at the front as Diamond dorm left their camp to find the Heart Tree.

"We're going to be really helpful," she whispered to Pearl. "We'll look really hard and find as many things on the list as we can while we ride. Then the others won't think I'm useless."

"You're definitely not useless," Pearl said. "You're great!"

"Thanks." Matilda stroked Pearl's neck, but she was still hurting from the others' words. Did Freya and Rosa really find her annoying, and did Ariana really think her drawings were just scribbles?

She swallowed. She wasn't used to feeling that her friends were unhappy with her.

"Is that Valentina?" Violet said suddenly. "What is she doing? And look at that chair!"

In the middle of a circle of trees, Valentina was sitting on a comfy blue chair that was padded with silver pillows. She was shouting out instructions to the other girls in Ruby dorm, who were busy running around her.

"Valentina, I've found something pink. It's up there, at the top of that tree. It looks like a feather from a rose finch," said Isla, a small girl with short brown hair.

"I don't want to just hear about it. Go and get it," said Valentina, bossily.

"But it's too high for me to climb."

Valentina stared up at the tree. "It is high, but Golden Briar can get it down with his wind magic. Where is he?"

"I'm here." Golden Briar was munching on a bucket of sky berries while the other unicorns were helping their girls. He wandered over. "You need my wind magic again? What for this time?"

Valentina and Golden Briar were second years. Golden Briar had found his magic last year, but since he hadn't bonded with Valentina, they hadn't been allowed to graduate.

"See that pink feather up there? Blow it down!" Valentina reached for a chocolate from the bag next to her. She made a face when she noticed Matilda and her roommates approaching. "I mean, I wish we could use your wind magic to get the feather," she said hurriedly. "But we can't because that would be cheating. And Ruby dorm would never cheat, would we, girls?"

Isla looked confused. "But earlier you said that using Golden Briar's magic wasn't cheating because—"

"Because we aren't going to use any magic," said Valentina loudly. "What are you staring at?" she added, glaring at Matilda. "Oh, I know. A successful team."

"A big fat cheating team, more like," said Matilda. "I know you were going to use Golden Briar's magic to get that feather."

"You can think what you like. You didn't see anything. And I'm not sure having magic would make any difference to your chances anyway, Matilda. Not unless it's super-strong tidying magic. I mean, look at the state of you. Do you even own a comb? Oh, don't tell me, I expect it broke in that bird's nest you call hair. Go away and take your loser friends with you. You're not going to win the scavenger hunt. We are!"

Matilda tensed.

"Ignore her," said Violet. "She's not worth it."

"You're right." Matilda breathed out slowly. "Let's go."

"Ruby dorm can't be allowed to cheat," said Ariana angrily, as Diamond dorm rode away.

"I know, it's not fair," Violet agreed. "But what can we do? If we tell the teachers, then we'll just look like tattletales."

"I think we should tell," said Rosa. "Cheating's wrong. What do you think, Freya? Freya, are you even listening?"

Freya was sitting on Honey's back, a faraway look in her eyes. "Yes, totally," she said, blinking. "Whatever you say."

Rosa sighed.

"I hate telling tales," said Matilda. "Let's not say anything. We'll just have to make sure that Diamond dorm wins."

"Yes, let's do that!" said Rosa, looking happier.

On the way to the middle of the woods, they

went around a pond, and Rosa found a sparkling hag stone in the water. Then Violet spotted a green feather caught on a branch.

"We're doing really well," she said. "We've got three things, and the chinchilla fur will make four."

"Wow!" Matilda said as they entered a huge clearing at the center of the dell. "Look at that!" The ancient Heart Tree was twice the size she'd expected. Caught in a ray of sunlight, its trunk shone pure gold and its thin branches curved overhead. But as Pearl walked closer, Matilda realized something was very wrong. The tree seemed to be covered with a furry mold, and instead of being red, the heart-shaped leaves were wrinkled and brown. Piles of dead leaves lay at the base of the tree.

"Is that really the Heart Tree?" asked Freya.

"It can't be," said Violet. "It's dying."

Matilda got off Pearl and went to look closer.

"It is the Heart Tree," she said, picking up a crinkled heart-shaped leaf from the ground.

"What's that noise?" Ariana had followed Matilda over to the Heart Tree, but now she stopped to listen.

"Look!" breathed Violet, pointing at the base of the tree. Dozens of scared, dark eyes were peering around the trunk at the girls and unicorns.

"It's the chinchillas!" said Matilda. She and the others dismounted and approached slowly. The chinchillas huddled closer together, chittering in worry. They were surrounded by piles of soft pink fur.

One brave chinchilla left the group and scampered toward the girls. It stood up on its hind legs and chattered at them, waving its little front legs.

"I don't understand chinchilla," Matilda said, looking around at the others. "But I'm pretty sure it's asking for our help!"

CHAPTER 6

Matilda moved closer to the chinchilla that seemed to be trying to talk to them. It squeaked in alarm and raced back to the others. They all scattered, their squeaks becoming more high-pitched as they jumped into the Heart Tree's drooping branches, sending more leaves swirling to the ground.

"Stop," called Matilda. "We're not going to hurt you. Please come back."

"They're terrified. Whisper, can you help?" asked Ariana.

Whisper had soothing magic. It meant he could calm animals and people whenever they were scared or angry. Tossing his mane, he lifted a hoof and stamped it on the ground.

Crack! Blue, pink, and purple sparks swirled in the air, carrying the scent of burnt sugar. A memory tugged at Matilda's mind. She'd recently smelled that same smell. When had it been?

But her thoughts were distracted by the chinchillas. As Whisper's magic reached them, they stopped squeaking and climbed back down to the base of the tree. Looking much calmer, they scampered toward the girls, who kneeled down to greet them.

The chinchillas jumped into their laps. Matilda ended up with one on each shoulder and three in her arms. Their soft pink fur tickled her chin, and their eyes were dark and sparkling. They had large round ears, and they made a soft chittering sound.

"What is it?" she whispered, knowing they were trying to tell her something. "What's been happening here?"

"I bet it's something to do with the Heart Tree," said Rosa, looking up from her own armfuls of chinchillas. "I wonder why it's dying."

"Hey, why are you all wearing chinchillas?" called a voice.

It was Miki and Himmat from Topaz dorm. Matilda smiled at them; she liked both of the boys.

"Is pink fur the new fashion?" said Himmat, laughing loudly.

"Shh, don't scare the chinchillas. Something's upset them," said Violet.

Miki and Himmat stopped fooling around right

away. "What do you mean?" Himmat asked, lowering his voice.

Rosa explained what they had found. Himmat looked at the tree while Miki, who was good with animals, picked up a chinchilla from the ground. He stroked it gently, starting behind its ears, then along its back and tail. The chinchilla relaxed into Miki's arms. Miki frowned. "Something's definitely wrong. Look how patchy its fur is in places. I know chinchillas molt at this time of year, but their coats should always look glossy and healthy. Himmat, can you pick me some leaves from those small white flowers? Yes, those ones," he added as Himmat pointed to a shady area dotted with tiny white star shapes.

"Everyone, try feeding the chinchillas these leaves," Miki urged as Himmat handed him a leaf and he offered it to his chinchilla. "They're good for chinchillas. They've got lots of the vitamins they need and help calm them down."

The chinchillas munched on the leaves, staring at the children with huge eyes as if they were waiting for them to do something.

Miki pushed his long black hair out of his eyes. "I don't understand. Whatever it is that's upsetting the chinchillas, it must be very serious for their coats to look like this."

"I think it's got to be something to do with the tree," said Violet.

"I vote we find Ms. Rivers and tell her about it," said Ariana.

"I agree," said Rosa, "but let's finish the scavenger hunt first and then tell her. A couple more hours won't make any difference. It would be so annoying to let Valentina win, especially since it sounds like she's cheating." Rosa put the chinchilla she was cuddling down at the base of the Heart Tree. Then she pulled a ball of pink fur from her top. "This will do for the scavenger hunt. Come on, let's get going. We'll help the chinchillas and collect some fur for Matilda to sleep on later."

"We'd better get going too," said Miki. He placed his chinchilla down and plucked some fur from the ground. "You're right, a few more hours won't matter. Hopefully, Ms. Rivers will be able to help. She knows lots about animals."

Everyone jumped back on their unicorns, but Matilda hesitated.

"Come on, Matilda," said Pearl, nudging her. But Matilda was longing to draw the Heart Tree.

"Just give me a few minutes," she begged, pulling her sketch pad out. "I'll catch up with you in a sec!" she called to the others, who had started riding away. "Don't wait!" She didn't want to stop them from finding the things they needed.

"Okay," Rosa called back. "Don't be long!"

Silence fell and Matilda started to draw. The tree looked so sad with its fallen leaves, but it was also still strangely beautiful. What had happened to it? Her fingers flew across the page. The chinchillas scampered around her feet, but then suddenly they froze, their large ears moving. Matilda listened, and then she heard it too—the sound of hoof beats. At once, the chinchillas fled. Scrambling over each other, they raced into the surrounding bushes.

"Matilda," said Pearl. "Look!"

Matilda followed Pearl's gaze and she gasped. A figure cloaked in black was cantering toward the clearing on a golden-maned unicorn. The unicorn's hoof beats grew louder as it carried the hooded figure closer. Icy fingers swept down Matilda's spine—was this the person responsible for the Heart Tree dying and the chinchillas' fear?

Matilda climbed onto Pearl's back, but it was too late for them to escape. She gripped Pearl's mane. "What are we going to do now?" she whispered.

CHAPTER 7

Pearl cantered toward a bright orange bush at the edge of the clearing. Its twisted leaves looked like a roaring fire. "It's too small to hide us both!" cried Matilda. "We need something bigger!"

Sparks shot up in front of them and a smell of burnt sugar filled the air. Matilda squeaked in surprise, and Pearl skidded to a stop as the bush suddenly doubled in size.

"What just happened?" gasped Matilda.

"It's my magic!" said Pearl. "Those sparks came from my hooves. I was wishing the bush was bigger, and suddenly it was!" She ran behind it. "I must have glamour magic—it means I can create illusions for a short time. My aunt has it too; it's awesome."

"Glamour magic! Oh, wow!" That explained all the strange things Matilda had seen recently—the wings, the sleeping bag. But she didn't have time to think any more about it. "Shh!" she hissed as she looked around the bush and saw the hooded figure cantering into the clearing. Matilda got off Pearl's back and kneeled behind the bush.

"Um, Matilda, I don't know how long I can hold the glamour for," Pearl whispered, her breath tickling Matilda's ear. "My aunt always told me it's hard to control a glamour at first. Stay as still as you can, that should make it easier for me."

Matilda nodded, pressing a finger to her lips. Her heart pounded loudly as she watched the person leap from their unicorn in a swirl of black cloth. Matilda tried to see their face, but the hood hid it well.

The figure glanced around and then walked over to the Heart Tree. They took out a round glass bottle from a bag tied at their waist and set it at the foot of the Heart Tree. Then they got something else from under their cloak. It flashed in the sunlight. Matilda almost gasped out loud. A knife! The figure made a long, deep cut in the tree's trunk. Tossing the knife on the ground, the figure lifted the bottle to the cut and caught the deep-red sap that oozed from the trunk.

Matilda could hardly watch as the magical sap dripped into the bottle. The tree's branches drooped even further as their life force drained away, leaving just a few stray drops glittering on the bark. If only she could see the figure. She leaned forward.

"Matilda!" Pearl whispered in alarm. "Don't move! The glamour's fading!"

Matilda's breath caught in her throat as the pretend bush hiding them started to tremble and disappear.

"Make another one!" hissed Matilda.

"I can't," Pearl panted. "My magic's not strong enough yet."

"Then gallop!" screamed Matilda, climbing onto Pearl as the figure glanced around. Pearl raced into the woods, heading for the track that led back to the campsite. Matilda looked back, expecting to see the dark figure and the unicorn with the golden mane chasing after them, but to her surprise she saw that the chinchillas had come out from the bushes and had leaped at the person's cloak, hanging on to it with tiny claws and running up the sleeves.

"No! Get off, you little pests!" It was a woman's voice, but Matilda didn't stop to hear any more. Leaning forward, she rode Pearl through the dense trees until they broke out onto the track. Matilda realized that Pearl was not galloping as fast as normal—doing magic had clearly tired her out.

"Keep going," Matilda said to her. "Come on, Pearl!" She stroked Pearl's neck, hoping her unicorn would feel her love. Finding an extra rush of energy, Pearl raced along the track, leaving the dark figure behind.

"Look! There's everyone up ahead." Matilda sat back, and Pearl slowed down. "We're safe now. I don't think they followed us. Well done, Pearl. You were amazing."

"So were you. You were really brave," panted Pearl. "Thanks for not panicking."

"It's my fault we nearly got caught. If only I hadn't moved, then you would have held the glamour and that horrible person would never have seen us."

"That's not true," said Pearl. "It's much easier to hold a glamour if you keep still, but I was already losing that one. It was my fault for not having better control of my magic yet."

"No. It's my fault, not yours," said Matilda. "I promise to listen more carefully in the future."

Matilda hugged Pearl's neck. "Thanks for being the best unicorn ever."

"And thanks for being the best friend a unicorn could have," said Pearl. She tossed her head. "Now let's go and tell the others what we saw!"

CHAPTER 8

Rosa was checking items off their scavenger hunt list while the rest of Diamond dorm held out their finds. Matilda and Pearl cantered into the center of the group.

"Oh, there you are, Matilda. We thought we were going to have to come back and get you. We've done really well—Freya found a six-petal daisy, so now all we need is an orange leaf. If we find one quickly, we could win!" Rosa finished excitedly.

"Are you okay?" Violet asked, seeing Matilda's pale face.

"There was a cloaked figure. She chased us!" Matilda blurted out.

The others frowned. "Really?" said Rosa.

"Is this one of your jokes, Matilda?" asked Ariana. "Because if it is, it's not very funny."

"Yes, we haven't really got time to joke now," said Freya.

"Not if we want to get back before Valentina's team," added Violet.

"I'm not making it up!" said Matilda. "It's true!" She told them everything that had just happened. She didn't leave anything out, even telling them the part when she'd not remembered to stay still and caused Pearl's glamour to collapse. "The chinchillas were great," she added. "They stopped the person from chasing us."

Ariana frowned. "You don't sound like you're teasing," she said.

"I'm not!" said Matilda. Why wouldn't her friends believe her?

"Matilda is telling the truth," said Pearl, backing her up.

"She must be!" Freya said. "Look, everyone!" She pointed at Matilda's hair. "Matilda's got a streak of pink and yellow in her hair. She's bonded with Pearl!"

Matilda tipped her head forward and stared in surprise at the pink-and-yellow lock of hair, the exact same shade as Pearl's mane. Happiness rushed through her. Now the others would have to believe her!

"Oh, wow!" said Rosa. "Glamour magic is so cool and useful too."

"Hang on," said Ariana. "If the story's true, shouldn't we be getting out of here? I can't imagine the chinchillas will be able to stop the person for long."

"Shh!" said Freya, suddenly holding up her hand. "Can anyone hear that?"

Right away, everyone stopped talking and listened.

"Hoof beats. Oh no! They did follow us!" Pearl's ears flickered in worry. "Quick, everyone, gallop!"

"Too late!" The golden-maned unicorn ran out from the trees, the hooded figure steering it straight toward the girls. Her voice, muffled by the cloak, was mean and angry. "This time I'll put an end to your nosy ways."

Her unicorn stopped in a shower of sparks. Lifting its hoof, it stamped on the ground. The earth started to move, flying up into a mini tornado of glittering red and yellow sparkles. The tornado buzzed as it spun toward the girls. Then, suddenly, it broke apart.

"Hex hornets!" yelled Matilda, as the huge,

angry insects flew at the girls and the unicorns. They all ran away in alarm. Hex hornets would chase people for hours and give them terrible stings.

The hex hornets reached Ariana and Whisper first. Whisper reared up in a panic, and Ariana screamed and tumbled off his back. As always, the island's magic formed a purple bubble around her, protecting her so she wasn't hurt. But as the bubble carried Ariana safely to the ground, the hex hornets surrounded Whisper, so she couldn't reach him.

The figure cackled with laughter. "Time for a little binding spell next, I think!" She began to pull something from her cloak as clouds of hex hornets buzzed toward the other girls. Pearl whinnied and turned to bolt away.

"Wait!" cried Matilda, looking back and seeing

the others all being surrounded. "We can't leave them! Do something, Pearl. Turn into a tiger or something."

"I can't," said Pearl, stopping. "I'm too tired for my magic to work."

"You can do it!" said Matilda, leaping off Pearl's back and seeing the figure riding toward Ariana with a hand stretched out. "You're totally great at everything!"

"Okay, I'll try." Pearl slammed her hoof on the ground. Sparks flew in the air and disappeared. The cloaked figure looked around and laughed loudly.

"How sad! You don't have any magic that can hurt me."

"You're the sad one, hurting innocent creatures!" screamed Matilda. "Try again, Pearl. You can do this. I know you can!"

Pearl took a deep breath and stamped so hard

the ground shook. Pink sparks shot up into the air, and suddenly Pearl vanished. In her place stood a giant orange-and-black-striped tiger with legs as thick as tree trunks. Matilda heard her roommates gasp and saw their astonished faces. The tiger threw back its head and roared, showing its huge teeth.

"Shape-shifting magic!" the figure said in horror. "Go!" she screamed to her unicorn. It ran through the trees, kicking up leaves and twigs as it raced away with Pearl, the tiger, chasing behind.

CHAPTER 9

Matilda watched happily as Pearl, disguised as a tiger, roared and sprinted after the panicked unicorn. She had no idea how Pearl was finding the energy to use her magic when she was already so tired. The cloaked figure and her unicorn crashed through the trees and disappeared from sight.

"Pearl," yelled Matilda. "You can stop now. They're gone!"

As Pearl slowed and turned back, her stripes faded and her body changed from a tiger with huge paws back to a unicorn with four hooves. Matilda realized the hornets had disappeared along with the cloaked person. A thought flashed across her mind: *Perhaps they have glamour magic too.*

Pearl walked back to Matilda, panting.

"That was incredible!" gasped Rosa.

"Wasn't it?" Matilda was glowing. "You were so brave, Pearl. I don't know how you did that when you were so tired."

"I did it because you believed in me. You gave me the faith to find more energy when I thought I had none left." Pearl pushed her head into Matilda's arms. Matilda hugged her tightly. "It was lucky the person thought I was a shape-shifter," Pearl went on. "If she'd realized it was just a glamour, she'd have known I couldn't really hurt her. My tiger teeth might have looked sharp, but they couldn't really hurt anyone."

"Which makes you even braver for chasing her away," said Matilda.

"I'm really tired now," said Pearl.

"We need sky berries," said Freya. "They'll help Pearl get her energy back."

"But we left them all at our camp," said Violet. "We left the heavy stuff there with the backpacks and tents—remember?"

"It's okay, I've got some," said Ariana. She opened up the small bag she'd been carrying. "I brought them with me just in case." She handed a pile of sky berries to Matilda, who fed them to Pearl until her breathing slowed down and she started to look better.

"Thank you," Matilda said. "I'm really glad you're always prepared for anything."

"That's okay. Thank you for saving me," Ariana replied. They smiled at each other. "I'm sorry I said your drawings were scribbles earlier," Ariana went on quickly.

"I didn't mean it at all. Your drawings are amazing. I was just upset about you forgetting your sleeping bag."

"I'm not surprised; it was stupid of me," Matilda said. "I should have read the list you gave me and made sure I had everything before we left." She looked around at her friends. "I promise I'll try to be more organized and less distracted by drawing from now on." She bit her bottom lip. "We're probably going to lose the scavenger hunt because of me. If I hadn't stopped to sketch the Heart Tree, we'd have been back by now."

"But then we wouldn't have found out about the person hurting the Heart Tree," said Rosa. "That's far more important than any contest. We need to get back and tell Ms. Rivers right away."

"Even though we still don't have everything for the scavenger hunt?" said Matilda. "You said we still needed an orange leaf, didn't you?"

"The safety of Unicorn Island is far more important than winning a scavenger hunt!" said Rosa. "I know I like to win, but the island comes first."

"Definitely. It's more important than anything. I think we should find Ms. Rivers as quickly as we can," said Freya, nodding.

"Okay." Matilda put her hand on Pearl's mane to climb onto her back.

"Matilda, what's that orange thing in your hair?" Pearl said suddenly.

"You mean the streak of hair that shows we've bonded?" said Matilda. "It's not orange, is it? Your mane is yellow and pink."

"I know that, silly! No—I mean, what's this? Look!" Pearl pulled a small orange leaf from Matilda's hair with her teeth.

"It must be from the bush we were hiding behind!" said Matilda.

Rosa clapped excitedly. "Matilda! You must have hidden behind a flame bush! That's the last thing we need for the scavenger hunt!"

"We can still win!" said Ariana.

"If we get back before anyone else," said Freya.

"What are we waiting for?" Matilda cried. "Let's go!"

★

They galloped all the way back to the teacher's campsite. Matilda didn't let herself get distracted by anything on the way back. There was no way she was going to be responsible for Diamond dorm not winning now!

As Pearl ran past the white tree at the entrance to the woods, Matilda saw the boys from Topaz dorm standing around Ms. Rivers, talking seriously. They must have gotten back first. Her heart sank.

Rosa and Crystal came to a stop beside Ms.

Rivers. "Did you beat us?" Rosa asked, looking at Miki and Himmat.

"No," said Miki. "We didn't read the list carefully and we forgot we needed a hag stone. We went back to the Heart Tree to get an orange leaf because Himmat remembered there was a flame bush there, but when we got there, we found that in the grass by the tree!"

He pointed to something in Ms. Rivers's hands. Matilda's eyes widened as she saw that it was a silver knife—the very same knife she had seen the cloaked figure using on the Heart Tree.

"I don't know what it was doing by the Heart Tree," Ms. Rivers said. "But I've sent a message to Ms. Nettles, and she's on her way here. The boys say the tree seems to be dying and—"

"I know what's happening!" Matilda blurted out.

For once, Ms. Rivers didn't scold her for

interrupting. "What do you mean, Matilda?" she asked.

The story tumbled out of Matilda's mouth. Everything she had seen: the cloaked figure with the knife in the clearing, the way she had chased Matilda and Pearl. The others chipped in too when it came to describing how she had found them and attacked them and how Pearl had scared her away.

Ms. Nettles and Ms. Bramble arrived when they were halfway through their story, and they had to tell it all over again.

All three teachers were looking very worried by the time the girls had finished.

"This person must be draining magic away from the Heart Tree," said Ms. Nettles. "The red liquid Matilda saw is its magical life force. The person who did this is very dangerous. Did you see her face, girls? Could you describe her?"

"No, she was covered by a cloak and a hood, and her voice was quite muffled," said Rosa.

"Can I see the knife, please?" said Ms. Bramble. Ms. Rivers passed it to her.

Ms. Bramble gasped. "But this is my knife!" She turned the silver knife over in her hands as she looked at it. "I locked it in the cupboard this morning after I'd been out with Ms. Willow fixing the quiverleaf tree. I have no idea how it got here."

"We will have to look into this," said Ms. Nettles.

"Do you think it's the same person who stopped the waterfall?" said Rosa.

"We will not waste time guessing without

any proof," said Ms. Nettles. "The two events may be linked or they may be totally unrelated. For now, our focus has to be saving the Heart Tree. Ms. Bramble, can you do anything for it?"

"I think so. I could also arrange for the gardeners to watch over it to prevent another attack, if you'd like me to. They will be able to protect the chinchillas too."

"That sounds like a very good idea," said Ms. Nettles. She sneezed loudly. "Excuse me, everyone, my hay fever is back. I will return to school, but I will ask the teachers to patrol Dingleberry Dell to make sure that everyone's safe during the night. We can talk more in the morning when the camping trip is over."

In the distance, there was the sound of galloping hooves. Matilda turned. Had the hooded figure returned? But as the hooves grew louder, she saw that it was a group of students riding toward them. The lead unicorn had a long golden mane and flowing tail, and its rider, Valentina, punched the air with a fist as she passed the white tree.

"We're back! I won! I mean—Ruby dorm won!" she quickly corrected herself.

She jumped from Golden Briar's back and then noticed everyone standing there. "What!" she said. "How come Topaz and Diamond dorm finished before us? Did you cheat? I bet you did," she said, glaring at Matilda.

Matilda held Valentina's eye. "Why would you think that?" she asked sweetly. "Diamond dorm are definitely not cheaters."

"No, we are not!" said her friends.

"Unlike other people around here," said Rosa, nudging Matilda.

Valentina glared at her.

"Let me check you have everything on the list, Diamond dorm," said Ms. Rivers. Rosa handed her the bag with everything in it. The teacher checked everything inside while Valentina folded her arms and muttered to her roommates.

"Well, I'm happy to declare that Diamond dorm are indeed the winners!" Ms. Rivers said.

"Gah!" Valentina said, her face now as sour as a lemon. She stomped away, leaving her roommates to shyly congratulate Matilda and her friends.

"Well done, girls," Ms. Rivers said to Diamond dorm.

Miki sighed. "We'd have won if we hadn't forgotten the hag stone."

"You should always read lists very carefully, Miki," said Matilda in a mock-strict voice.

Ariana squealed happily. "Now, that's something I never thought I'd hear you say, Matilda!"

Matilda grinned. "Well, I guess I've learned stuff today." She looked around at all her friends. "And not just that I need to be a bit more organized in the future. I've learned how amazing my unicorn is, how great all my friends are, and how much I love having fun with them all!"

Ms. Rivers's face softened. "Then I'd advise you to go and keep having fun," she said. "You all definitely deserve it. Let me get your prize for winning." She fetched two bags of huge pink and white marshmallows and gave them to Matilda.

"Yum!" said Freya.

Matilda handed one bag to Miki. "Here," she said. "I think Topaz dorm should have this."

He fist-bumped her. "Cool, thanks!"

"Now off you go back to your campsites," said Ms. Rivers. "Oh, and if anyone has forgotten anything, now is the time to say so. I have extras of most things. Matilda, is there something you're missing, maybe?"

"Um, my sleeping bag," said Matilda.

"What? You mean this one?" said Ms. Rivers, going to her tent and pulling out a purple sleeping bag.

Matilda gaped. "How did you know?"

"I did a quick check of the stables before we left," said Ms. Rivers, some of her usual strictness creeping back into her face. "I didn't tell you earlier because I thought that if it slowed your team down, then it might teach you a valuable lesson."

"It did," said Matilda. "And I won't forget it."

She grinned at Ms. Rivers as she took the sleeping bag. "Thank you."

"Now go on! Shoo!" said Ms. Rivers, flapping her hands at them.

★

It wasn't long before the girls and their unicorns were settled in their camp. The unicorns munched on sky berries while the girls organized the camp and set up a roaring campfire. Matilda wanted to make some sketches so that she could paint the scene later, but she resisted and put her sketch pad inside her sleeping bag. She worked with everyone else, doing her fair share of the chores. It wasn't long before everything was neat and tidy. Ariana let out a happy sigh. "Shall we toast the marshmallows now?"

"Yes, let's!" said Matilda, going to get the long toasting forks that Ariana had packed.

They sat around the campfire, listening to the

hiss of the flames as the marshmallows turned soft and gooey.

"I love camping," said Violet.

"Me too," said Rosa.

"This is quite fun," said Freya. "It's actually nice taking a break from my invention. What?! Where's the fire gone?" she said as she found herself toasting her marshmallow over an icy water fountain.

"Pearl!" Matilda giggled as she looked around to see that her unicorn had crept up behind them.

"Busted!" Pearl said. She stamped her hoof and the water fountain turned back into flickering red-and-gold flames.

"Your magic's so cool!" said Violet.

"How about this?" said Pearl. Looking at Ariana's tent, she stamped her hoof. It turned into a miniature castle with turrets, flags, and a drawbridge.

"Oh, that's so pretty. I wish I could sleep in that tonight!" said Ariana.

"I don't think I can hold the glamour for a whole night!" As Pearl spoke, the castle became a tent with a turret at one end. There were shouts of laughter as it slowly faded to reveal the normal tent.

Matilda blew on a toasted marshmallow, then popped it into her mouth. As it melted on her tongue, she felt incredibly happy. She loved studying at Unicorn Academy. She'd made a great bunch of friends, and Pearl was the very best unicorn.

"I meant what I said earlier," she told her friends as she stuck another marshmallow on her toasting fork. "From now on, I'm going to try to be more organized. And I'm going to stop joking around so much. It was horrible when you didn't believe me about the hooded figure."

"Well, don't change too much," said Rosa, giving Matilda a hug. "We like you the way you are."

"Yes, don't get too sensible," said Ariana.

Matilda grinned. "I don't think there's much chance of that!"

"Group hug," said Violet. "Come on, Freya. That means you too!"

Freya rolled her eyes. "Really?" she grumbled, but she got up to join in the group hug. "The others are right. You're not that bad," she added quietly to Matilda.

"Aw, thanks," said Matilda, bumping her cheek against Freya's.

"Who wants hot chocolate?" asked Violet, breaking away. "We can float some of the marshmallows on top."

As everyone made hot chocolate and toasted more marshmallows, Pearl nudged Matilda.

"The others are right; don't change too much, Matilda. I love you the way you are. You're my perfect partner."

"And you're mine," Matilda wrapped her arms around Pearl's neck and hugged her tightly. "I'm so lucky to have you!"

She looked up and saw a huge sparkly red heart hanging in the sky. She rubbed her eyes, and when she looked again she saw it was just the moon.

"Pearl!" She giggled.

Pearl blinked at her, her dark eyes sparkling like the stars overhead. "Friends forever?" she said.

"Forever!" Matilda declared.

"Matilda, where are you?" called Violet. "The hot chocolate's ready."

"Coming!" Matilda kissed Pearl, and with her heart full, she ran to join her friends.

Freya still hasn't bonded with
her unicorn, Honey, and Freya is
getting worried. Will they find
Honey's magic and finally bond?

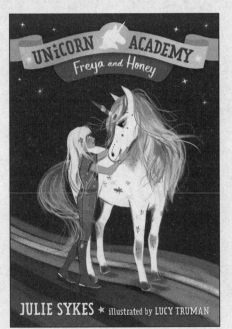

Read on for a peek at the next book
in the Unicorn Academy series!

"Come on, Honey!" cried Freya as Honey, her unicorn, weaved in and out of a row of upright poles. Circling around the final pole, Honey raced toward a table with two beanbags on it and a large hoop on the ground. Freya could hear her friends from Diamond dorm cheering them on.

"Go, Freya! Go, Honey!"

"You're in the lead! We can win!"

"Miss the hoop!" chanted the boys from Topaz dorm as Honey skidded to a halt by the table. Freya ignored them. Leaning down and grabbing the first beanbag, she aimed carefully and threw it into the hoop on the ground. Honey nudged the next beanbag closer to Freya's hand with her nose, and Freya threw that one into the hoop too. "Thanks!" she gasped as Honey set off, galloping toward a tall tube standing in the grass.

It was a Sunday afternoon, and Diamond and Topaz dorms were holding an obstacle race at Unicorn Academy. The two dorms got along really well and hung out a lot. They'd set the course up together. The fastest to finish would win, but time was being added on for every mistake each unicorn-and-rider pair made. So far, Honey and Freya hadn't gotten anything wrong!

Reaching the tube, Freya climbed down from Honey's back. She'd been looking forward to this challenge! The tube had a small white ball inside it, and the rider had to somehow get the ball out of the tube without touching it and put it into a cup. There were two long-handled spoons beside the tube. Everyone else had taken a long time to remove the ball using only the spoons, because they kept dropping it. Freya loved making things work, so this was her kind of challenge.

"I need water!" she told Honey as she dismounted. "Can you get some from the bird bath? As much as you can!"

Not stopping to ask why, Honey galloped to the bird bath, filled her mouth, and galloped back.

Freya pointed to the tube. "In there, Honey!"

Honey spat a stream of water into the tube. As the tube filled up, the ball was pushed upward. When it reached the top, Freya scooped it out with one of the spoons and tossed it into the cup. It had taken almost no time at all.

"We did it!" she cried, jumping onto Honey's back.

The two of them raced across the finish line with Honey's long red-and-gold mane and tail streaming out behind her.

"Freya won!" shouted Rosa, who had been timing Freya's round along with Miki from Topaz dorm. "Diamond dorm are the best!" she whooped.

Freya and Honey were quickly surrounded by the rest of Diamond dorm and their unicorns.

"That was amazing!" said Matilda, throwing her arms around Freya. Freya wriggled away. She didn't really like hugging or being hugged.

"You were so smart on that last challenge," said Ariana.

"I can't believe you thought to use water to get the ball out," Violet agreed.

Freya grinned. "It was fun, wasn't it, Honey?"

Honey whinnied in agreement.

"Rematch!" shouted Himmat from Topaz dorm. "Let's go again."

"Okay," said Rosa. "You're on!"

"Count me out," said Freya. "It's been great, but I've got stuff to do."

"Your big secret invention?" asked Violet.

Freya nodded.

"Oh," Honey complained. "Can't we stay, Freya? Please? You can work on your invention another time."

"No, I really need to work on it now," Freya said, dismounting and giving Honey a pat. "You can stay, though." Honey didn't know that Freya's secret project was a present for her birthday, which was in just three days. Freya still had a lot of work to do on it.

"It won't be the same without you," Honey said, nudging her with her nose. "Please stay?"

But Freya had to go. She said goodbye and hurried back through the gardens toward the school. Her invention—a robotic unicorn that would bring Honey treats whenever she wanted—had been inspired by the automatic carts that moved hay bales around the stables. It had seemed the perfect way for Freya to combine her engineering skills with showing Honey how much she loved her. She couldn't wait to see Honey's reaction when she saw it!

Maybe she'll be so pleased we'll even bond, thought Freya hopefully. All the students at Unicorn Academy were paired with a unicorn when they first arrived, and they spent a year at the academy training to be guardians of wonderful Unicorn Island. During that year, the unicorn usually discovered their special magic power and bonded with their rider. Rosa, Ariana, and Matilda in Diamond dorm had already found their unicorns' powers and bonded with them, but Freya and Honey and Violet and Twinkle were still waiting.

Freya hurried toward the school, her mind focused on her invention. When she was near the end of a project, it was like having an itch she couldn't scratch until it was done. There were just a few problems to fix now. The robot was working, but it still wasn't moving properly. *I need to keep it from bumping into things and spinning to the left*, she thought. *But how?*

The buildings of Unicorn Academy looked beautiful in the golden autumn sunlight. The marble and glass school glittered brightly, but Freya barely noticed. Deep in thought, she headed for the little room next to the art studio that she had been using for her invention. It was time to get to work again!

★ ★ ★

New friends. New adventures.
Find a new series . . . just for you!

ISADORA MOON

For ballerina and fairy and vampire lovers

MAGIC ON THE MAP

For adventurers

UNICORN ACADEMY

For unicorn lovers

PUPPY PIRATES

For dog lovers

PURRMAIDS

For mermaid and cat lovers

BALLPARK Mysteries

For sports fans

RHCB rhcbooks.com

Every Isadora Moon adventure is totally unique!